AF488470

Books by McKay Smith

*Arcane Inkblots*

*Broken Halls*

*Press Start to Play*

# BROKEN HALLS

A Make Your Own Journey Story

By McKay Smith

Realmbreaker Press |

# Dedication

*To Colton,*
*for taking a chance on me,*
*and helping me believe*
*that I could be a writer.*
*Thanks,*
*–MS*

# Important Notice!

This book isn't like a normal book that you read from start to finish. At the end of each chapter, you will have to make a decision and follow the page number it tells you to go to.

**For example:**
Go through the door on **page 1.**

Climb the stairs on **page 125.**

If you wanted to go through the door, you would go to **page 1** and see what happens.

Good luck and enjoy *Broken Halls!*
–*M.S.*

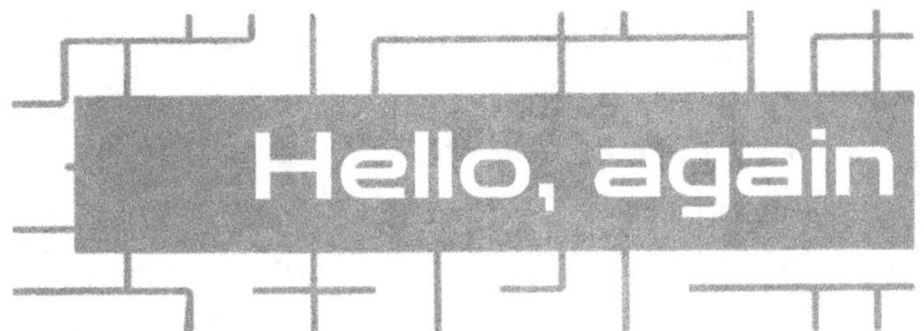


Buzzing fluorescent lights hum overhead, a sound too familiar to be comforting. Dusty sheetrock walls, their simple yellow-white wash barely concealing old wallpaper. You've been here before, haven't you?

Your head pounds, the world spinning like a rickety carnival ride as you strain to remember . . . well, anything.

A stench hangs in the air, your nose tugging on the strings of memory. Something not unpleasant, but old and musty.

So terribly familiar. Yet you can't remember when you were last here. Or where here even is. The world sharpens. The hallway stretches in both directions, branching into dim passageways.

From where you stand, you can't see where they lead. The place looks unkempt with scratch marks on the walls and dead flies in the lights. No

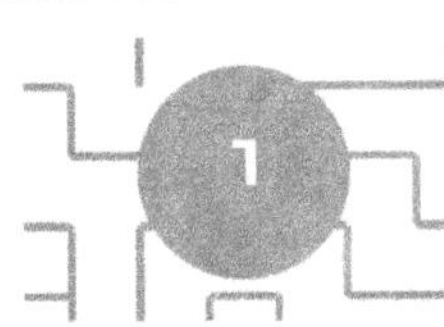

one has passed through here in a long time, unless it's like your office building, which always looks neglected.

The green shag carpet squishes underfoot, and your footprints leave clear impressions. But there aren't any other footprints.

Your throat feels raw as sandpaper.

Even breathing scrapes it, each inhale causing pain. You need water. Soon. But where?

You dive deeper. Each passage branches off again and again, seemingly nonsensical, each step increasingly confounding. No markings. No signs. You walk. Then run. Yet everything looks the same. Frustration burns. The pain in your throat demands relief.

You collapse, the weight of it all buckling your knees, pleading to the One Above for liberation. The silence sharpens, leaving only the hum of the lights, your only friend in these empty halls.

Maybe you should wait. Someone has to be here, right? Someone paying for the electricity? Yes. They'll come for you.

More than anything, you just want to be home.

Wherever that is.

Sitting on the ground is oddly comforting after the endless running. The squishy carpet welcomes you, plush and deep. Your eyelids sag . . .

A sharp, metallic scrape jolts you from your slumber. Heavy, wet, close breathing follows. You aren't alone anymore. But whatever it is . . . doesn't sound human.

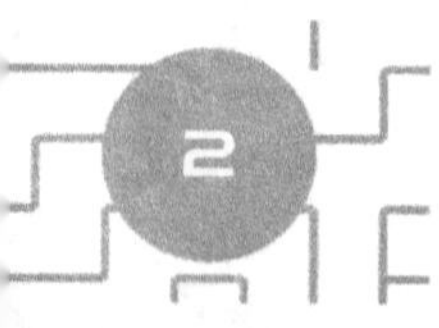

Your mind offers one thought:

Run.

Stumbling upright, you notice your footprints are gone. How long were you out? Where did you come from?

Your heart slams in your chest. Your head pounds. Your throat screams for water. But survival overrides it all. That thing is drawing closer.

Run. Again, the thought, but where?

You'd hoped rest would clear your mind. But no. Nothing makes sense in this forsaken place. The creature's footsteps are upon you.

You bolt. Walls blur. You scan desperately for any sign of salvation.

Nothing.

No one can save you.

No hope . . .

A plan sparks.

Two, actually.

One chaotic. One careful.

The first: run at random. Wild, desperate, without logic. Randomness got you through college exams, and you have the degree to prove it. Maybe chaos will mean freedom now.

The second: trace the wall. Build a mental map.

Try to escape the loops. Maybe even hide, if you could get that lucky.

Unless . . .

It is a circle.

It can't be a circle.

Right?

*Right?*
Behind you, the scraping only grows louder.
What will you do?

If you choose to run wildly, go to **page 5.**

If you choose to trace the wall, go to **page 8.**

# Run, Run, Run

Left, right, up, down. You have no idea where you're going. If you had run this fast in high school, you would have been a track star.

The building is a disaster. Staircases lead nowhere. The hallways slope and buckle, making it impossible to maintain a steady footing.

After what feels like forever, especially as you realize how out of shape you are, you finally stop. The metallic scraping is gone. You aren't sure if the creature ever pursued you. Still, your heart is pounding, and your throat burns from the ragged breathing.

You rest against a wall, sighing. Practicing those HR breathing exercises you always mocked, you calm your pulse. Huh. Who knew? Maybe HR did something right for once?

In the relative silence, a sound rises. Something strange, yet wonderful? Rushing water. Not like any mechanical, but natural. Like a river.

You blink. Are you dreaming? Did you pass out? A dying hallucination, only for you to wake with the beast hanging over you?

There can't be a river in the middle of a building.

But the sound is real, calling through your exhaustion. Desperation overpowers reason. You roll over and crawl toward it. Eyelids droop, vision flickers, and your ears are your only guide.

Turning a corner, your hands come across something new. Solid rock. Cool, smooth to the touch, worn down by the water. You force your eyes open.

You're in a cavern.

What?

Behind you, the hallway still stretches, but ahead is a vast underground chamber. Pale, luminescent moss glows softly, casting light on hidden majesty.

A rushing waterfall, emptying into a crystalline pool, just feet away.

Somewhere primal stirs. You scramble to the edge like a madman, scooping the water into your mouth.

At first, you choke, but it turns to blessed relief.

You splash your face, your chest, your arms. The coolness clings to you.

You breathe freely.

Paradise is relative, and right now, this is it.

Basking in the light and coolness of the waterfall, your body finally crashes.

Just a few moments of rest, that's all. The beast is far away. You're safe.

A few minutes couldn't hurt.

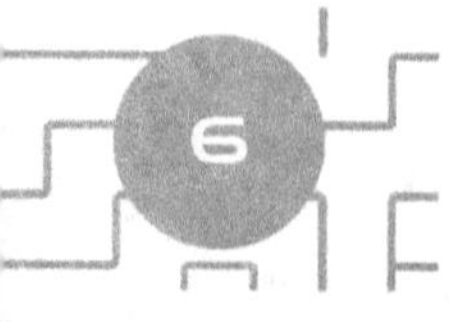

And you are so very tired.

Maybe you should keep moving. There's a real chance the exit isn't far. You might even start to understand this strange, new world.

The choice is yours.

Do you rest by the pool? Go to **page 11.**

If you go exploring, go to **page 13.**

# A Circle?

Tracing the wall, you quickly realize something is very wrong. In theory, you should have looped back by now.

But you haven't.

The floor isn't quite level, but you couldn't have reached a different floor ... could you? It's almost like the building is alive, reshaping itself to trap you.

No. That's ridiculous. More likely, your haste to escape the beast has thrown off your judgment and direction.

The creature's sounds have vanished. Was it even chasing you?

Maybe this is the same hallway. Maybe you weren't noticing the right details.

Yes ... that must be it.

Now, calmer, you begin to focus. Near some water damage, a piece of wallpaper is peeling. Along

the floor, there's a section of splintered wooden trim.

A childhood memory surfaces. You grew up a rebel, but that troublesome nature might now save your life.

You tear a section of wallpaper free. Kicking the trim, you break off a pencil-sized shard. You test it, scratching the wood softly on the wallpaper. It leaves a mark. Like when you were a kid.

You chuckle. Back then, you thought you were the next Van Gogh. Your parents didn't agree.

Drawing carefully, you sketch a crude map. It's surprisingly nostalgic. Comforting. The wallpaper, the scratching . . . it feels like home.

The memory sparks a warmth in your chest. Purpose. A hope of freedom.

It vanishes in a heartbeat, but it leaves an imprint on your soul. Almost like a familiar voice, urging you forward.

You press on. Your throat burns, screaming for relief, but now you have direction.

As you dive deeper, your map reveals how uneven this building really is. What first seemed like a single floor is actually two or even three. With the map, you can finally tell the hallways apart. Still, not a single soul greets you. Your footprints are alone, briefly visible in the green shag carpet before they fade too.

No scratches. No mark of the beast. Nothing.

You tear more wallpaper, adding to your increasingly convoluted map. Your unease grows. These hallways don't go to rooms or exits. It's a

tangled mess. More buzzing lights. More details to add to your map and anxiety.

Your thirst grows deadly. Your throat is so dry that the air itself is sandpaper against it.

Worse still, your collection of wallpaper is growing out of control. Rooms that you know you marked are pristine when you return. Is the building repairing itself? Or are you losing your mind?

You claw your throat. You need water. Now.

Frustrated, you rip a larger piece of wallpaper and attempt to merge your maps into one. Your vision blurs. Your head throbs.

Maybe the beast should find you. Your pencil tears a hole in your map, ripping it in two.

You want to scream, but your instincts stop you.

You want to cry, but your eyes are too dry.

You slump to the floor. You try to hold on to the warmth, that fleeting sense of home. It slips away like water, drowned out by the humming lights and creeping cold. What will you do?

If you decide to give the map one more shot, go to **page 15.**

If you want to toss the map aside and give up, go to **page 19.**

The stone doesn't make a comfortable bed, but you wake up feeling more rested than you have in a long time.

The ambience of the cave is refreshing and wonderful, almost better than some of the luxury spas you'd won through work. Maybe this place isn't as bad as you thought.

As you stretch and twist, cracking your back with a satisfying snap, you notice something is wrong. The room is darker now. The water isn't as loud, and everything feels muted.

Your heart starts to race uncontrollably, as if it will rip from your chest. Your hands shake, and a cold shiver runs down your spine.

Abruptly, a large, hulking shadow looms over you and the stone around you. You feel deep, heavy breathing brush the back of your neck. Two dark violet eyes stare down at you, their gaze pulling at

your very soul. An inhuman chill freezes your blood and stops your heart.

The world goes black as the beast grabs you, thrusting you into the icy water. Sound vanishes. Even the sensation of the water fades.

You resist, but it's futile. The creature only tightens its grip, dragging you deeper. You're shocked at how far the pool goes. The darkness presses in.

A deep, metallic laughter, like thousands of nails falling down a concrete staircase, breaks the silence. It sounds distorted by the water, yet unmistakable. It draws close, but soon the laughter entirely disappears.

The world is too quiet.

Your final sight is a blackness that consumes you.

Do you accept your watery grave and let your story end?

Or do you return, answering the call of the land of the living? Go to **page 1**.

# Exploring

Your eyes fill with wonder as you venture deeper into the caves. The space is impossibly vast, stretching farther than you could have imagined, with no glimpse of the outside world. Not a crack or window, absolutely nothing to let in natural light. The cavern feels natural in some places, but in others, it's shaped or carved. Something man-made.

Or at least, made by something. Ancient maybe? Or possibly supernatural?

Your throat itches again, but it's manageable, especially now you've found the waterfall. But when you turn around, you realize you can't remember how to get back. The cave walls all look similar, yet something about them has changed. They're less green, with less of the glowing moss. And yet, the space remains lit.

The moss was never the source of the light. Maybe it's the rocks themselves, pulsing and glowing?

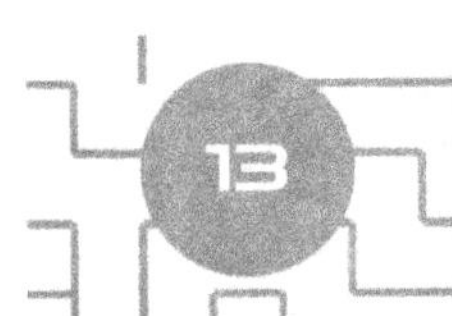

How odd. You want to stay as far away from the walls, for now.

If you were a scientist before, you'd be experimenting, probably trying to make sense of it. You feel curious about this place—but not obsessively.

Who were you before? And why does it feel like a part of you has been taken away from you?

The cave widens again, opening into an oddly familiar space. It's not the same place you saw the waterfall, but you've been here before.

Somehow . . . it feels like home.

Something about . . . your family? The sound of laughter, someone smiling at you . . .

No memory comes.

You explore further, and the space breaks off in two directions.

One has the familiar hum of sterile, electric light. An office building hallway, eerily similar to the one you woke up in.

The other leads to an ancient, heavy door. Its metal lock has mostly broken off, the hinges straining to hold it in place. No one has been here recently, but the broken lock appears recent.

Whoever came through . . . they were determined. Desperate. What were they running from?

If you enter the door, go to **page 21.**

Or do you return to the familiar on **page 19?**

You're exhausted. But you can still try one more time. Maybe it's the hope sparked by the memory, or maybe just your stubbornness, but you take a deep breath, channel your thirst, and pick up the scraps of the wallpaper, carefully tracing your maps.

The work takes your mind off your thirst as you lose yourself in the drawings. Rather than letting the situation feel completely out of your control, you find joy in persevering. Between your fourth and second maps, you notice something: a single hallway you somehow missed in all your exploring. You double-check the other maps. How had you overlooked it? But there it is.

Is it really possible?

Gathering your collection of maps and holding your new master map, you retrace your steps until you come to the entryway. It looks no different from the dozen others, but it is simply unmarked on all of your

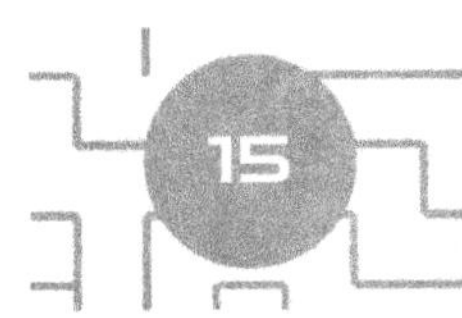

maps. You start down it and see something impossible.

A wooden door, with cheap plastic blinds draped over the window. Exactly like what you'd find in an office building. Your office building. A memory flashes by, but it's gone before you can hold onto it.

You try the handle. It's unlocked. The room opens to a heavenly sight:

An office water cooler.

With little paper cups.

You rush over, barely restraining yourself from crushing the cup in your hand. The water comes out slowly, filling it, and you swallow it in one gulp. Not nearly enough.

Tossing the cup aside, you realize there's no need for moderation. You can drink that holy nectar straight from the spout. It runs down your neck, soaking your shirt. You don't care.

Water has never tasted so good.

Later, when you reflect, you'll be sure there was a heavenly chorus singing praises.

Once your thirst is quenched and you're drenched, you take a look around. The room is simple. A potted plant. An overfilled trash can. A generic painting that no one knows the artist of, but everyone feels like they have seen before. Probably at a thrift store.

In other words, it was a standard office break room. *Your* office break room. Something clicks. You remember. After a stressful day at work, you come here to chat with coworkers. Not just coworkers, but friends. You'd commiserate during the week, complain

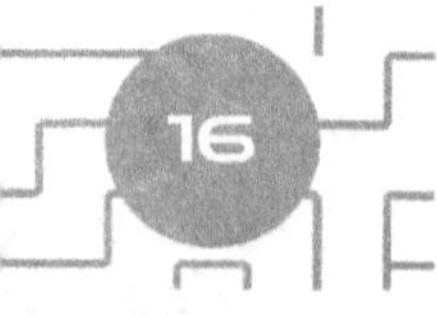

about everything, then party until dawn on weekends, only to drag yourself back on Monday
and do it all over again.

You smile as a tear runs down your cheek. It felt terrible at the time, but now, there's something wonderful about it. Such a simpler life, before . . .

. . . before what?

Reality creeps back. Memory fades. You're still in the break room. It's frustrating. The answers feel so close, yet still out of reach.

At least you're not dying of thirst. You can think clearly. Better keep exploring.

There are two doors, excluding the one you entered. They look almost identical—same cheap blinds, same windows. Both are unlocked.

You open one door and step into a familiar boardroom. A long table. Papers scattered across the surface. Plush office chairs encircle it, fancier than the ones in your cubicle. Only the best for the board members. You spot a few more doors. One, you remember, leads to the CEO's office.

Before your curiosity about the papers takes over, you check the other door.

It leads to a waiting room. A large couch welcomes you. Soft piano music plays. And finally, you're not alone with just the noise of your thoughts.

The light switch is dimmable. There's a small waterfall gurgling in the corner.

Thank goodness that you didn't find this room first. Your animalistic thirst might've destroyed that poor waterfall.

A wave of exhaustion washes over you. How long has it been since you've slept?

Your thirst is gone. Maybe it's time to rest. That's the healthy thing to do.

You're pretty sure you snuck off to sleep on this couch during work hours. An oddly comforting thought.

The water cooler is nearby. When you wake up, you'll be able to drink more and feel refreshed for whatever comes next. Those papers will still be there. It's not like anyone else is in the building.

Just let yourself rest.

Do you rest on the couch? Go to **page 26.**

Or look at the papers? Go to **page 29.**

You start down the broken halls as the glow of the fluorescent lights turns more sinister. What once felt familiar now seems haunting and hollow. The buzzing overhead reminds you of a dentist's drill. It pierces your skull.

The endless passageways blur together, and your growing thirst consumes your focus.

The world spins. The pain in your head swells, almost unbearable.

How did you come here? Was this some cruel joke? Some divine judgement that the One Above found necessary to inflict?

Something clicks. A church with beautiful stained-glass windows glowing in the sun. Laughter with friends on a sunny day. Warmth, someone holding you close, whispering words of peace. Hallucinations, probably, from the lack of water or fatigue. But still, there's beauty in it.

You steady yourself. You remember: you still have a choice. Don't give up.

Do you follow the walls to **page 8?**

Or do you run to **page 24?**

As you push on the wooden door, it splinters beneath your fingertips. With some effort, you force the remains open, showering yourself with dust and wood chips.

The new room is a dungeon, with an old, musty scent. Not too far from how your old office smells. Maybe that's something you should bring up to HR. Empty cages line the walls. The floor is damp and squishy.

Weak torches light the room, casting twisting, flickering shadows. You hear rats scurrying through the refuse.

Not long ago, that would have sent you running and shrieking your head off. Now you're just glad to hear something alive that isn't trying to kill you.

You feel unsettled as you examine the cells. Fresh food lies in the muck. The cells were recently vacated. You shiver. Where are the people?

You walk over and shake the metal bars. They're remarkably solid. You run your fingers along them and find reinforcements at top and bottom.

Curious. Strangely, the keyhole is only a few inches off the ground, nearly buried in grime.

The dungeon stretches the length of the hall, with maybe twenty cells in total. Near the end of the hall, a wooden door is by a winding staircase. Light spills from the floor above. Broken shelves sag with rotten books, soggy and unreadable in the water.

You try the door: Unlocked. It takes some effort to open, but you force it open and hear the pop of a seal breaking.

The room is dry and stale. Clearly, no one has been here for a long time. Papers lie scattered on the desk, in what looks like reformed chicken scratch., like your handwriting.

No, your handwriting is worse. Maybe 'orderly' reformed chicken scratch would be a more precise term.

Some appear to be maps, though none of the places you recognize. One shows a large building with several rooms crossed out in bold red Xs.

You pocket the map. On the wall, a ring of keys hangs. Probably keys to the cells, but others are too large or too small. You take them all.

Back in the main room, it's noticeably darker. The shadows seem thicker. Are the torches dying, or something else?

Upstairs, light pours through the floorboards, and you can hear the crackling of a large fireplace.

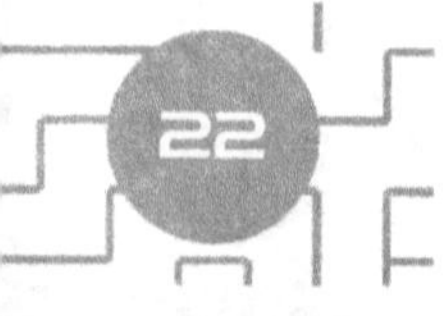

Do you keep searching the cells and uncover whatever secrets they might hold? Or do you head upstairs and continue your journey?

If you search the cells, head to **page 32.**

If you climb up the stairs, ascend to **page 35.**

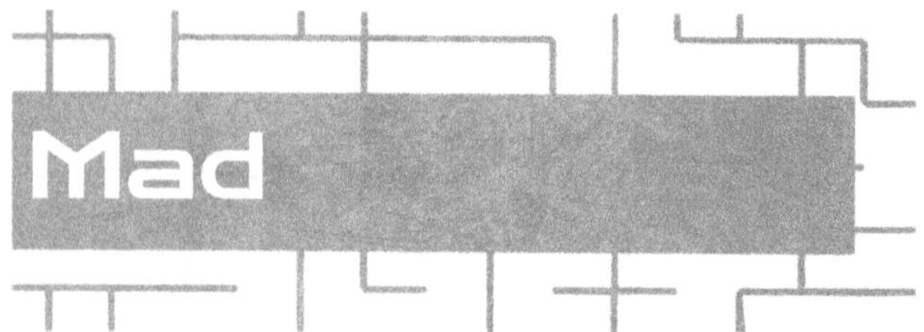

# Mad

You dash through the halls, simply not caring anymore. Hope? Faith? Ridiculous ideas. Logic will always win. That tells you that these passageways can't go on forever.

Right?

The minutes pass like water as you run. Or has it been hours already? Or only a few seconds? Still no windows, and the halls look more alike. Day. Night. Pointless. The world is on fire and ending, and *you don't care.*

Everything in your life is now these hallways.

You live and breathe them. You are these halls. Your throat burns. You don't care. Your legs that scream they'll collapse. You don't care. Your heart threatens to break. *You don't care.* You will find freedom.

You're not going in circles. But you need to be sure. More marks. Yes. You drag your fingernails along the wall, scraping lines in each room you pass. Faster now. Running now. Your proof. Your map. Time passes, or doesn't. You move forward. You can't lose momentum now.

You never see the same mark twice. But you've doubled back at least once. Right?

Your body feels weak. Steps falter, and you collapse, sliding to the ground. Splintered nails dig one last mark into the wall.

Your drive doesn't die. Escape could be around the next corner. So you crawl. Turning the corner, you find a room covered with scratch marks. Countless. And familiar? They couldn't all be yours. Could they? These were the markings of a madman. And you're not mad.

Are you?

You curl up on the floor, holding yourself together. Time stops mattering. You welcome the shadow hanging over you. Darkness fills your vision along with two glowing, violet eyes. Hot breath washes your face. The beast reaches for you. Fingers wrap around your chest.

You found one form of escape, didn't you?

Does your journey will come to an end?

Or do you rise once more, going to **page 1?**

You never fall asleep to music, but the cheap-sounding piano melody makes a surprisingly soothing lullaby. After running for so long, you probably could've slept on the floor, but you reward yourself with the couch. Your body sinks in. You get comfortable.

Besides, after inspecting the door more closely, you notice that it has a push-in lock. No one's disturbing your nap.

It all feels so good on your aching bones. You reach the light switch, flick it off, and drift off to dreamland.

And what strange dreams they are.

You are somewhere down south on a hot summer day. Heat rises off the pavement, and you're skateboarding with a couple of friends. You don't remember skateboarding before, but in the dream, you're a legend. The board feels like an extension of

your body, each trick flawless. A crowd cheers you on. It's perfect.

One by one, the crowd vanishes. Each voice cut out as if someone hit the remote mute button. Your friends keep skating, farther and farther away. You call for them to wait up, but they're gone.

Daylight dims. A chill sets in. You can't feel things in dreams, right? But the world is quiet now. Too quiet. Beat. Beat. Your heart pulse.

Panic builds. Beat. Beat. Beat. Run. Escape. They're coming. A shadow looms overhead. Deep, guttural laughter echoes in the distance.

You try to keep skating, but your movements turn sluggish. A crack in the road sends you flying.

The shadow engulfs you. Darkness closes in. Two violet eyes glow in the void. You're not sure when you started screaming, but no sound comes out. Your voice burns your lungs. The abyss welcomes you. Everything becomes an eternal night.

You jolt awake, panting. Light. You need light. Flicking the switch, it's just a dream. A horrible, horrible dream. But only a dream.

Maybe a sip of water will help.

As you head toward the door, you notice a figure outside the frosted glass. The blinds hide most of it, but something massive breathes slow and raspy just beyond.

It knocks. You back away as the shadow under your feet stretches, impossibly long. The room grows darker. Blackness coils around you, leaving no escape.

The door handle rattles. Metal twists and screams.

Silence. Darkness. Laughter. The same as your dream. Deep. Cold. Familiar.

Two violet eyes meet yours. You feel them pull at your very soul.

"Good night," an inhuman voice says. "Sweet dreams."

Is this the end?

Or do you fight once more? Go to **page 1.**

Your curious nature wins out, and you return to the boardroom. Taking a seat in one of the chairs, you stretch out and notice an AC remote on the table. You click it on, surprised to find that it still works. The cool air feels calming as you settle to pore over the papers.

Studying them, you're grateful to find they're in a language that you can understand. They detail an experiment.

Scientist were researching drawing energy from other worlds to power. . . something. Countless references to humans, but what were they trying to power inside humans?

Wait. You were part of this. Grasping at the edges of your memories . . . they were figuring out how to power life. Immortality.

With renewed vigor, you tear through the papers. The project was late in development, but they were on the verge of testing . . .

You rush to another stack of papers that has something that catches your eye. Photos. No. No. No. There!

A photo of you, underneath written: Subject 42.

Your hands shake as you hold the photo. You look thin. Stress. Something is bothering you. The other photos share the same haunted expressions.

You shouldn't be the only one here. Something went wrong. Horribly wrong. Where is everyone? Why is this building empty? Devoid of all life. Then again, that isn't much different than when you worked here.

Wait. Grabbing onto the memory, it is more distinct than anything you've recalled. In this very board room, the scientists explained the risks of the experiment to you. Every little detail, even the chance of otherworldly
interferences.

There was something unique about you, they said. Each of the candidates was distinct, of course. But you were special. You might've been the key to immortality. Clearly, fate had other plans.

Scrape! You jolt up from the memory. Something is clawing at the door, followed by a low, heavy breathing. A dark shadow looms in the door's window. The clawing turns shrill, like nails on a chalkboard.

You rush over, shoving a chair beneath the door handle, trying to jam it shut. Crash! Bang! The door rattles. You pile the chairs and tables. The flying papers form a haphazard tower, blocking your view of the glass.

BANG! BANG! The beast is relentless. You skim

the papers, looking for anything on the monster. The noise makes it hard to focus on anything. You need time. CRACK! The door is splintering beneath the beast's strength. It's out for blood. But why? Why does it hunt you?

Think. Something is there, just past your grasp, about the beast. But nothing comes. Your mind is blank. You scream.

Come on! One more memory. There has to be . . .

Escape routes. You'll take it. There are two exits from here you can picture: a fire escape and the CEO's office.

The fire escape is your best bet, as the CEO's office is probably a dead end. Yet, you've heard things about him.

He was eccentric. He made plans for everything from earthquakes to robberies. Also zombie apocalypses and sea animal tornados. Secret passages. He would disappear into his own office for hours. Maybe just rumors. Could you stake your life on that?

BANG! CRACK! Your makeshift barricade is breaking. The fire escape. Or the CEO's office. Guaranteed safety. Almost certain death.

The breathing is seeping through the cracks. Close. Too close.

SNAP! The decision is now or never.

The fire escape? Go to **page 37.**

Or the CEO's office? Go to **page 40.**

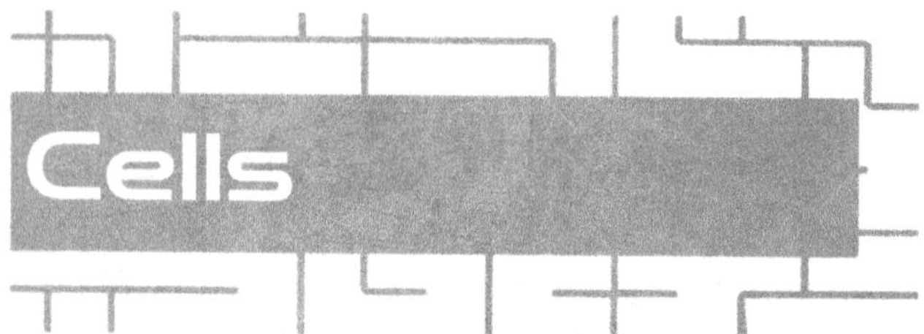

# Cells

There's always time. That's what Dad always used to say. His words are all you have left of him. You loved that man. You're not alone.

Rushing over, you slide the keys into the lock. The first one you try fits perfectly, smoothly unlocking the door. Not even a hint of rust. The door swings open like it's on ice, and you shiver. The air inside is unnaturally drafty and cold.

An uncomfortable crunch greets you as you step inside the cell. Best not to think about that. Or how thin your shoes are and how long it's been since you changed your socks. It will be even worse before you can change them again.

The thought sends chills down your spine.

Lifting your foot, there's another crunch. You gag.

No, no, no. Focus on the draft. Where is it coming from? Keep telling yourself that, and everything will be okay. Crunch.

The stones on the far wall look solid, but as you get closer, the breeze sharpens. You wave your hand in the air, noticing that the breeze forms a rectangle. Or maybe a door?

In the darkness, you trace the outline with your fingertips. An unfortunate squishiness greets you. Thick and damp, like moss but somewhat softer?

It can't be the worst thing you've touched today.

You rip it away, thin slivers of light shining through the cracks. Daylight. It's not enough to fill the room, but it feels glorious on your skin. Real daylight. You search for a handle or anything that will bring you closer to freedom.

How do you open this stupid wall?

You want to scream. The outside world is a stranger, but you know that you can become friends again if you could only find this ridiculous handle.

Who even makes a secret door in a jail cell?

Movies always have them, but why? Who designs a jail cell and thinks, "You know, what this needs? A secret door right here."

Someone who doesn't have faith in job security, that's who.

If only you had a little more light . . . Wait. Of course you do. The light in the hallway isn't electric.

You peek out of the cell and see dozens of torches. Why don't we use torches anymore? We wouldn't waste electricity by leaving the light on. Your mom wouldn't get after you anymore.

That brings a smile, but also a longing for home.

Under the torchlight, the shadows flee away, and

your eyes have to adjust. The crackle and warmth remind you of winters by Grandma's fire.

You see that the wall is . . . just a wall. There might be some scuff marks on the floor, but you're not sure. It might be a trap as a prisoner's final torment.

A deep, rumbling howl shakes the walls, sending dust cascading from the ceiling. The beast has found its prey once more.

Your heart pounds in your ears. This cell is a deathtrap. This whole room is a deathtrap. There are only two exits, and the monster is coming from one of them.

You curse. You have to run. Abandoning whatever this is. Freedom. Maybe something worse. If you only had more time. Just a little more time. Why won't it open? The perfect hiding place if you could only get the cursed wall open. Just a little more time . . .

The sound of claws is close. Too close. Choose now, or die.

Do you stay in the cell? Go to **page 42**.

Or do you run? Go to **page 44**.

The stairs are cramped. You keep tripping, your toes cursing the day that you were born. Eventually, you stumble your way to the top, finding yourself in a vast banquet hall.

Fireplaces crackle across the room. The room is opulent with long mahogany tables and golden dinnerware fit for a king. Candles float in the air, defying all physics, but you don't care. Only one thing is on your mind.

That delicious smell of food. There are plates set for hundreds, and you are starving. Nothing looks familiar, but your stomach doesn't care. You position yourself in the middle of the room to keep watch on the many entrances and dive in. As a kid, you were a picky eater. Not anymore. Definitely not today.

The variety of food is endless. It's warm, fresh, and divine. Flavor bursts in your mouth. With hints of savory, sweet, and deep, rich, umami, the food is divine.

Your throat now demands relief. The goblet's thick, syrupy liquid warms and fills your stomach. You let out a belch, unrestrained in your solitude, close your eyes, and relish in the moment.

Time slips by. You remain undisturbed. After you've had your fill, your curiosity takes hold. Between all the exits and entrances in the room, two catch your eye.

Near the head of the banquet, a feastmaster's table lies untouched by time. Behind it, there's a large, beautiful hardwood door. Intricately carved, each shape made with the finest detail. Could those carvings hold some answers about this place?

On the room's far side, a smaller, metal door draws your attention. A single metal figure is embedded in it, forged so precisely that it almost disappears in the design of the door. It seems to call to you.

If you enter the wooden door, go to **page 79.**

If you choose the metal door, head to **page 81.**

You let curiosity die and survival win. Curiosity killed the cat, and you're not eager to test that theory. Bursting through the exit, leaving papers behind, you make your escape.

*CRASH! BANG!* The sounds erupt as you slam the door behind you. Your blockade of chairs and tables must have exploded across the room. Hopefully, that buys you enough time.

The fire escape appears unchanged. You'd gone down it a couple of times. The company ran a handful of drills, far below the legal regulations. Always right before the fire marshal came, so they'd always pass.

The abyss stretching beneath the escape is definitely new. But it's better than certain death with the beast.

*BANG!* Another crash shakes the door.

Time to move. Even if it means running straight into the unknown.

The exterior walls emit a soft, bluish glow, highlighting the darkness flowing around you.

Was it fog?

The beast crashes onto the escape. You bolt down the rickety stairs, two or three at a time, your heart hammering. The metal shakes beneath your feet. You trip and catch yourself against the wall.

The building changes from concrete and steel to cool, uneven stones. The air becomes moist and heavy. You hear water dripping in the distance.

The beast isn't pursuing you anymore. At least not down the escape.

You push yourself to your feet and notice that you're standing in the middle of a cave. You step off the last few rungs, your feet landing in a shallow puddle. An ominous splash echoes through the cavern.

Still no beast.

There's a faint buzzing. Something electrical. To your left, a hallway stretches out, almost identical to the ones from earlier. Is this another endless prison? Or a way out?

To your right is an ancient door, carved straight into the stone. It catches you eye.

The texture rugged with scratches and dents running along the grain of the wood, dust clogs its grooves, untouched for years.

The puddle beneath you connects to a thin stream trickling from the door. Moving water is safer to drink, but you don't want to risk it. That stuff looks like it would give you a parasite with world domination on its agenda.

What's the plan? Choose the right and enter the ancient door? Or left and returning to the cursed building?

If you enter the mysterious door, go to **page 21.**

Or do you return to the building on **page 19?**

# The Office

You burst into the CEO's office, papers slipping from your hands as you slam the door closed. A roar reverberates through the office, followed by the sound of wood snapping and crushing.

You quickly scan the room. On the desk, a red button blinks softly, the light reflecting off its glass casing.

That's worth a shot.

Lifting the glass, you slam the button. With a satisfying click, the room erupts. Metal bars crash down over the windows, shrieking like iron banshees. A thick metal sheet slams over the door, vibrating the floor. Flashing red lights appear from hidden compartments. The air smells sharp and electric. A robotic voice blares, *"DEFCON 1 protocol engaged,"* the sound vibrating against your chest.

Eccentric was an understatement; the CEO was insane. His paranoia was saving your life, so maybe you shouldn't complain. As the chaos settles, you take stock of the room.

Beneath the harsh red glow, it's strangely normal. A desk with a family photo, a file cabinet in the corner, two drawers jammed closed. Dust floats in the air from your disturbance. The lights hum, almost soothing compared to the harsh hallway lights.

CRASH! The metal groans, vibrating from the impact. You jump, adrenaline spiking, but the door holds firm. This room could withstand the zombie apocalypse. Nothing breaks through that easily.

Wait. Something is missing.

A critical part of any hideout from the undead. You head to the filing cabinet and yank one of the broken drawers. It screeches in protest, metal scraping against metal, but finally, it snaps open. Papers scatter like leaves to reveal polished wood and cold steel. A shotgun. And ammo. The weight is solid, comforting in your hands.

Zombie movies, the ones your crazy uncle loved and showed you over the summer, taught that no zombie shelter is complete without a trusty shotgun.

It's universally acknowledged. Nothing stops zombies like shotguns. Hopefully, it'll work on the beast as well.

Do you open the door and blast through **page 64?**

Or do you explore the bunker further on **page 66?**

# A Kick

You growl and kick the wall hard. The first lesson your old man had taught you about car repair was one you'd never forget.

Click. A section of the wall falls, revealing a narrow hole. You mutter a quick thanks to the One Above as you shove a key from the key ring into the lock. The brickwork smoothly slides apart to reveal a door. You rush inside, slamming the door and locking it behind you.

As you twist the key, something heavy crashes against the door. Dust spirals around you. A low, rumbling growl chills your bones, but further pounding leads to no avail. That was close.

But where are you now?

The room opens to a grand antechamber. Ancient paintings line the walls, each depicting knights in gleaming armor. Far above, daylight filters through a stained glass window, casting vibrant streaks of color on the stone floor. Gentle wind chimes tinkle faintly in the breeze.

After the hellscape that you have been living in, the view takes your breath away. For the first time in forever, peace warms your heart. You reach a small waterfall, dip your fingertips in, embracing the coolness. It empties into a river flowing beneath the secret door, becoming the source of the dungeon's water

It's crystal-clear, reflecting the multicolored rays in brilliant patterns. The beauty is such a stark contrast from the haunting, damp dungeon, transformed into something almost heavenly.

People are like that. In the wrong light, they seem monstrous. But, with a new perspective, they become beautiful, even extraordinary.

The river bends around a stone dais. A brilliant, gleaming sword, driven into the stone, calls to you. It's a mystical sight, reminiscent of your father's fantasy stories from your childhood. A lost age, filled with knights and chivalry, and a forgotten, divinely chosen king destined to redeem his people and to bring hope in the darkness.

An almost impossible hope in our world.

You reach for the sword, but stop. Is it a trap? Is the beast luring you in? Or is this freedom for you and everyone else?

Do you take the sword and go to **page 46?**

Or leave it on **page 48?**

# No Way Out

Forget secret doors! You need to escape with your life. Tossing the torch aside, you break into a dead run, heading away from the beast's furious growls.

There's a horrible, crunching noise beneath your feet, mirrored by another further down the hall, the beast. The sound echoes off the stone walls, amplifying tenfold like a hundred creatures are chasing you.

The hallway stretches endlessly as you approach the staircase. As you pass the jailer's room, your body feels like it's moving through molasses. Your feet stop in place, the world freezing. Against your better judgment, you steal a glance behind.

A dense, suffocating darkness surrounds you. A murky taste fills your mouth. All light gone, the room plunged into silence.

A chill settles around you, and the blackness touches your skin, parasitically leeching into your

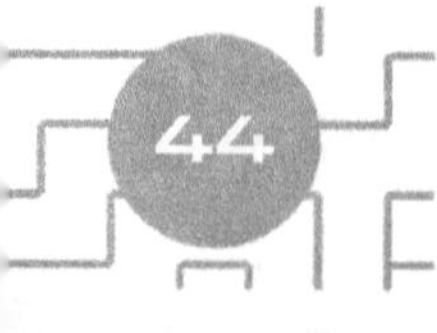

flesh. You turn back to the staircase, but it's gone, replaced with only blackness.

For a moment, the molasses grip eases. You bolt, but the ground is slick. You slip, crashing down with a sickening crunch. Bitter, icy water floods your mouth. The taste is foul.

No. You try to push off the ground, only to collapse again, swallowing another mouthful of the filthy water. You slam your fists against the wet ground, water splashing everywhere. It's hopeless. There is no escape from this cursed place.

The splashing stops. Your hands still flail, but there's no sound. Nothing. Silence drowns the world.

You look up.

Two violet eyes, glowing faintly, stare back at you. You try to turn away, but the eyes follow, locking onto your gaze.

"There you are," says a chilling, inhuman whisper. The voice slices through the silence. "Why must we play this game?"

A jump. A gasp. A scream.

Blackness consumes you.

Do you let it end your story?

Or do you go back to the light? Go to **page 1.**

Stepping up to the stone, daylight pours onto your face, warm and blinding. The darkness in your bones flees, removed by the sun's returning embrace. Like your hometown's spring coming after an eternal winter.

Dawn has broken into your life once more. You reach forth and grasp the sword's hilt. The metal is smooth and cool beneath your fingertips. A bear runs the length of it, the carving almost lifelike, jaw opening to the sword's blade.

You pull it from the stone, surprised by how easy it slides free. The warmth of coming home after a long journey abroad channels through you. This sword is your destiny.

The blade catches the sunlight and gleams, scattering light in every direction. Not a speck of dust, it shines as if freshly polished from the master's hand.

Vigor surges within you. Whatever beast has

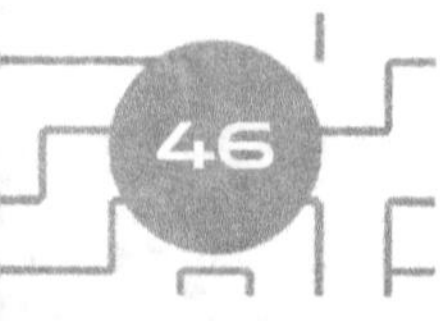

hunted you, its rain of terror ends now. Wherever this place is, it's yours now. Your domain. Your chaos. You linger in the moment, as long as you dare, and step down. A sheath lies at your feet.

It's a perfect match. Was that there before? You strap it to your back, and the weight gives you a new determination. It becomes an extension of your body, another limb you can use.

Let the games begin. Down the passageway, there's a polished metal door. It's unlocked, and inside is a nice bunker. A wooden bed and plush mattress greet you. Locks and deadbolts line the door's interior, providing a safe place to rest.

An inhuman shriek rips through the air, echoing down the hall and into the bunker. It comes from the direction of the antechamber.

Claws scrape against stone, like nails on a chalkboard, followed by heavy, ragged breathing. The sound is drawing close.

What do you do?

Do you hide out in the room on **page 50**?

Or do you face off against the beast on **page 53**?

You take one last look at the sword, soaking every last detail, but leave it. A trap. Maybe. You can't take the risk, even if it's straight out of your dreams.

Besides, you've barely explored this room. You wander. There's so much more to see.

A hallway calls to you. There's a slight, dusty breeze in the air. Its floor has a sprawling mosaic of a bear, crafted with hundreds of stones, each carefully shaped by the master's hand. Even weathered, it's stunning and majestic. A fortress worthy of a king.

Where are the people?

A memory flashes before your eyes: you, nestled in your mom's lap as a kid. You couldn't be more than five or six, snuggled up to her, reading books about knights and castles. You'd dream of visiting the old country, and after finishing school, you took a trip. Tears fall as the memory blurs your mother's face. You wipe it away.

*Are you in the old country?* It doesn't look familiar, but there are hundreds of foreign castles

Down the hallway, a blue light flickers. It starts as a pinprick but gradually expands. A single tone vibrates in your chest, growing in intensity as you near the source.

It's the strangest thing you've seen yet. There's a black and smooth wall, radiating with blue light. The tone swelled into a simple song, familiar and strange.

You reach forward, surprised to find the wall is nonexistent—your hand slipping right into the blackness.

Is this the way out? An escape to freedom?

You step forward onto **page 68.**

You slam the door and lock the dozen bolts behind you. Almost instantly, the beast violently slams against it. The door holds firm as this bunker could withstand a military siege. Finally, a true safe room.

Taking a deep breath, peace washes over you. The pounding continues, but as time passes, it fades into the background, dulled by your mind. Probably best to wait it out. You stretch out on the bed, laying the sword on the nightstand.

Exhaustion crashes over you. How long has it been since you actually slept? You easily drift into strange, vibrant dreams.

You are with your parents as words are exchanged, but it's garbled and distorted. Everything is impossible to make out, besides your feelings. There's passion in the room, and you remember a deep, sinking frustration.

A thousand times you tried. A thousand times,

they wouldn't listen. They refused to trust you about an experiment. Salvation for them, for everyone in the world. A glorious purpose, providing real meaning to your life, after a deep darkness.

Angry, you left. Slamming the door, not even saying goodbye. The dream shifts. You're in the car, crying.

Deep down, you knew that they worried because they loved you. You might never see them again, leaving you wishing you had said goodbye.

You never did.

You wake suddenly. The pounding is gone, replaced by an electric hum. You feel a chill, but you're unsure if it's from the room or your dream.

Your eyes are crusted with dry tears, the memory lingering like a shadow. Groggy, you sit up and scan the room. The locks are in place, the door untouched. But something new is in the room.

A mini fridge.

You approach it, the humming growing louder. It's definitely electric, but there are no power cables. How in the world is it getting power? There's not a single outlet in the room. You try to move it around, but it's impossibly heavy. How did it get here?

The front is mostly bare, except for a few papers and magnets. One is a workplace safety regulations flyer. It's probably been unread since it was mandatorily slapped on the front.

A magnet of Smokey the Bear snapping a giant matchstick catches your eye as well. Something about it feels familiar, but you can't quite place it.

You are afraid of where it might lead, but you are also incredibly curious. Plus, it might have food, and you are starving more than a Boy Scout after a day at summer camp.

Do you open it on **page 55?**

Or do you leave it be on **page 77?**

Unsheathing the sword, you step out of the safe room. No turning back now. You are done waiting. Done hiding. Done running.

It's time to escape. To leave this cursed prison. You're the hunter now. And your prey awaits. The hallway dims. Shadows pour into the hall, seeping through the cracks in the wall. You pause. The darkness thickens, pooling into every corner.

Two violet eyes flare in the blackness. Heavy breathing caresses your neck. You take a torch, flickering in the creeping dark.

You hold it high, straining to glimpse your foe, finding only darkness. The torchlight fades, the fire sucked dry by the shadows. Its crackle dies, leaving silence.

Low and steady breathing breaks it, followed by the scrape of claws, digging into the stones, the noise of the earth itself ripping apart.

"There you are." The gravelly voice freezes you. Somewhat human, but twisted and so horribly wrong."Taking what isn't yours. What you can't possibly understand."

Each word hammers into your skull. It's close and metallic like steel grinding into a tin roof. Soulless. Lifeless.

"I'll kill you, as I have done a thousand times." Memories surge through your mind. Other lives, trapped in this same building. One after another, slaughtered by this beast's hand. Terrible deaths as your soul is torn from your body, only to be stitched back together by some unholy force. Hot tears burn against your cheeks.

How long has it been? How long have you been hunted by this beast? The pain almost stops you dead.

No. Not this time. You will not let this monster rob one more second of your life. You find strength and raise your sword. This has to be the end. You must stop the cycle. Turning towards the voice, darkness swallows the rest of your vision. Only the violet eyes remain, piercing your soul.

"What will it be this time?" It asks, voice dripping with cruel glee. "Let's play a game."

Do you strike? Go to **page 57.**

Or do you hold back? Go to **page 59.**

Your gut tells you the fridge is the best option. Maybe that's just hunger talking, but your instincts haven't led you astray yet. You crack open the door.

A cool breeze hits you. Inside, there's oriental takeout, some mysterious food in a container that would definitely kill you, and some water bottles. In other words, your standard office mini fridge.

The takeout calls to you. You've always been a sucker for it, and even cold, it tastes divine. Cracking open one of the water bottles, you wash down the saltiness with icy gulps. The mystery of the fridge lingers, but you're not complaining. It's a gift from the One Above.

The rest of the room remains unchanged, and the door stands firm, remaining unmarked from the earlier beating. A thought crosses your mind. If the fridge couldn't have come from anywhere else, the only logical explanation is that it came from below.

You grip the fridge, remembering a self-defense maneuver from a class in high school. With a twist and a pivot, you slide it from its place. It's surprisingly light, suggesting whatever was in those horrid containers wasn't a black hole of death, as you first assumed.

There are things you've found in workplace fridges that have scarred you for life. Beneath the fridge, a murky blackness pools. You scoop some with your hand, only to have it trickle back into the pool without a ripple. It's cool to the touch, robbing heat from your hand.

You try stepping into it, but there's no purchase beneath its deep surface.

Do you dive in on **page 68?**

Or abandon the pool on **page 77?**

You strike with everything that you have left. Every ounce of rage, desperation, and the raw desire to escape. The sword connects, slicing into the beast, who unleashes an ear-piercing shriek.

Fighting the urge to recoil from the awful noise, you dig in deeper, driving the blade until you connect with the floor. You hold it, unyielding, until the creature stills and the shrieking ceases.

You pull the sword back. A dark liquid sprays across the floor, splattering the floor with a sickening *drip-drip*. Your breath is ragged, but eventually your pulse slows, leaving you in silence.

Did you win? Is the beast dead? The darkness remains, thick and unyielding, making it impossible to tell. You want to shout, scream in victory, but your voice is caught in your throat.

You try again, but no noise escapes. Something is horribly wrong.

The floor shifts, turning to quicksand, sucking you down, pulling you into the depths. The walls press in, becoming suffocating. You never thought yourself claustrophobic until now.

Every sound in the room disappears. No dripping. No footsteps. You can't even hear your own breath. Or the beating of your heart.

"Idiot."

The voice splinters the silence. It's not just one voice. It's a hundred metallic whispers scraping against your bones, rumbling through your soul.

"I cannot be killed."

The room erupts in a cursed light as dozens of different colored glowing eyes blink into existence. They trace your every move, unblinking, unrelenting.

Sharp pin pricks dance down your spine, the darkness suffocating you, squeezing the air from your lungs.

You gasp, but no air comes. Your blood runs cold, your heart turns to ice. You shut your eyes, desperate to block out the horror.

"That won't do at all."

Some pries at your eyelids, forcing you to ahead. A wall of shining white teeth surrounds you. Waiting.

"Goodbye, brave little hero. See you again soon."

Is this the last goodbye?

Or do you rise once more on **page 1?**

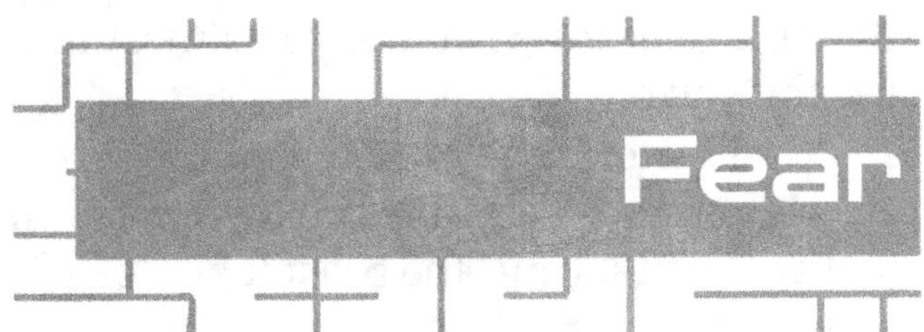


"Are you scared?" the beast hisses.

In the suffocating darkness, with all your senses deprived, something builds inside of you.

A warmth deep in your soul, unlike anything you have felt before.

Words of comfort echo in your mind. Spoken by a friend on a rainy day. *Light will come in the morning,* he had said. *No matter how long the night may seem.*

The world can take family, friends, everything. But it can't take the light of a new day.

Hope. A hope that cannot be killed.

You open your eyes, confidence swelling. You stare straight into those violet eyes.

"I don't fear you." Your voice is barely a whisper, but the words kindle a fire in your bones.

"What?"

"I. Don't. Fear. You. Anymore." The fire grows, stoked by the light of your soul.

"Impossible," The beast spits, voice shaking. "I am TERROR."

The words try to freeze and stop you, but they can't touch the fire inside. You remember your friend's smile, and you can swear you can almost hear him cheering you on.

"You're nothing!" You scream.

Light floods back into the room, radiating from you. For the first time, the beast takes form in your vision.

"No! Stop! This isn't how our game goes." The beast recoils, shrinking as you step forward. "You can't win. You will never escape!"

"No. I choose! This is my fate!" You raise the sword, the blade radiating with brilliant light. "Your hunt ends now!"

The beast stands before you, an amalgamation of fur and bones, eyes and arms in all the wrong places. Claws jut out at odd angles, and a rancid stench fills the air. What had once seemed great and terrifying is now small and pathetic.

"You can't see me like this! I am—"

You strike, driving the sword cleanly through what you believe is the head.  The entire creature explodes into a mist of darkness, evaporating with a final, pitiful wail.

"You're finished."

You sheath the sword, surprised to find it unscathed. The torchlight flickers back to life even brighter than before.

At the end of the passage, a different kind of light

glows. Natural light. *Daylight.* A light that you never thought you would see again. You can feel the warmth on your skin.

A way out. Go to **page 62.**

You walk towards the light.

The warmth is now a waterfall. The outside world unfolds into a transcendent cityscape. People mill around, taxis honk, and a comforting chaos of busyness fills the streets. Tears fill your eyes as the realization sinks in: You escaped.

You're free from that awful hell. Memories crash over you like waves. You remember the experiment "The Great Purpose." It was to provide a cure to death itself. Immortality freely given to millions, fueled by siphoning energy from dying realities. A select few were chosen, you among them.

Until everything had gone horribly wrong.

The other realities proved unstable and fragile. The office building, the one that had been your recent prison, had become a lightning rod to the universe, fusing with the broken shards of those other worlds.

You remember waking up in the rubble of the

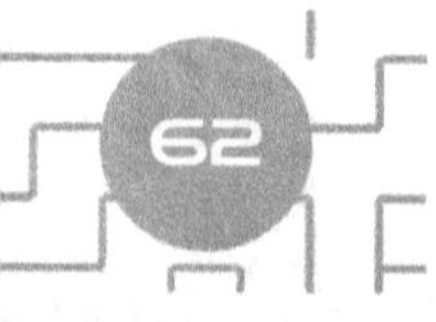

laboratory, your companions dead. Except for him. One scientist had survived, but at a terrible cost. He became the beast.

That was the beginning of the game. An endless cycle of immortals, hunter and prey. Until now.

You keep walking, your steps gaining confidence. The streets of New Rex City stretch before you. As dust leaves your memories, you realize you're only a couple of blocks away from your apartment.

Your family could be waiting for you.

Hopefully, they're still alive and haven't forgotten about you. Or given up on you.

No.

If you know one thing about your family, it's that they'll never give up on you. No matter what you do, they will be waiting. Open arms with unwavering love.

You start running.

To home.

**The End.**

# Blasting

Channelling the spirit of your crazy uncle, you slam the DEFCON button once more. As the room shifts back in place, you lock and load the shotgun. Adiós to the beast and hola to freedom.

The metal grinds open to reveal a door filled with spiderwebbed splinters. You step back and position yourself behind the desk, using it as a makeshift barricade.

*CRASH!* The door cracks spread, jagged and creeping. *CRASH!* A chunk of the door bursts free and shatters midair. The jagged hole left behind is swallowed by darkness.

Wasn't the boardroom lit before? Did the beast kill the lights?

You glance around. The lights are dimming, almost like they're being drained by the hole's void. A violet eye blazes in the darkness, fixated on you.

*BANG.* No demon eyes today. You fire straight at

the hole. The blast is deafening, but you don't hesitate. You pump the gun, aim, and fire again.

*BANG.* A second for good measure. Your ears reel in pain. *BANG.* If the zombie movies taught you anything, it's that the supernatural is stubborn. You can't be too careful.

Gun smoke curls around the room, masking your vision. Your ears ring with the echo of the shots. The beast has to be dead. Right?

The smoke clears, revealing only darkness. Every light in the room is gone. The ringing in your ears fades, replaced by . . . nothing? Did you deafen yourself?

Hopefully, it's not permanent.

"It won't be," says a deep, metallic voice.

Your heart stops. You fire the shotgun twice more in the direction of the voice, but this time there's no sound. No explosion. No recoil. Just . . . silence. Wait. There's heavy breathing. But not your own.

"See you soon, old friend."

Something pierces your chest, stealing your breath. Your vision blurs, the world slips into blackness. You cling to one last thought: Will you let this be the end?

Or will you return and fight again on **page 1?**

Maybe going all out on this creature like a dude from those zombie movies wasn't the best idea. That rarely ends well for the people in those situations.

Besides, if you've learned anything about zombie shelters, it's that they always have multiple escape routes. Unless it's the one at the end of the movie, where they're trapped and die a slow, painful death as the zombie hordes break in.

You shudder. Hopefully, this isn't one of those.

The filing cabinet didn't let you down before, so you might take a second look. You try pushing it, straining against the weight, but it barely budges.

Shifting your stance, you throw yourself against it. Still nothing. No matter the angle, it's concrete.

But when you use the back wall for leverage, it slides with startling ease, revealing a passageway.

Narrow stairs spiral down into near-darkness. *THUNK!*

Another crash shakes the metal door. Although you trust it to hold, it's time to get moving. Grabbing the shotgun, you step into the passageway. The stairs lead you down farther than you expect, each level sinking deeper into shadow.

At the bottom, there's a small trapdoor with its latch undone. You crack it open, thick blackness spilling out. You can't tell how far it goes.

Curious, or maybe just stupid, you reach your hand inside. The darkness spills into your palm like liquid. It trickles between your fingers, leaving icy pinpricks in its wake. Across from you, something unexpected: an elevator, with polished doors. An "Up" button glows faintly in the dim light. You push it.

The doors open smoothly. A cold breeze brushes your face. The interior is immaculate with spotless floors and mirrored walls. There are no other buttons. Just a flashing arrow pointing up.

It's quiet. Soundproof, from what you can tell. No one to hear you scream. Not like there's anyone left, anyway.

You can't recall passing another elevator during your descent, so you're clueless about where this one leads. You've come to a crossroads. What path will you take?

The trapdoor? Go to **page 68.**

Or the elevator? Go to **page 70.**

# Dark Portal

Descending into the blackness, you're struck by a chill. You fall, faster and faster, but there's nothing to see, only the sensation of wind passing you. You reach out, grasping at the emptiness, but your hands find nothing. All your possessions disappear in the void.

In the silence, a memory resurfaces. A voice, warning you and the other participants about the experiment's dangers. They said it would change the world as a solution to death. A world free from fear and suffering.

It was dangerous, yes, but was there a nobler cause? You did it for your family, but they push you away. Why wouldn't they trust you?

Did you push yourself away?

A scream.

Panic. Darkness.

Suddenly, your feet connect with something solid. There's no pain. The fall ends softly, almost like

you're floating. You stand there, suspended in blackness. What were you thinking about? Where are you? The darkness clears and . . .

Go to **page 1.**

# Elevator

You decide that the elevator is the better option, leaving the strange trapdoor behind. Inside, the entire room is spotless, and for the first time in forever, you see your reflection in the mirror. You look awful, like someone ran you over a half dozen times with the latest John Deere model and dragged you the rest of the way across their field.

Maybe it's better you're alone right now. You couldn't live with someone seeing you like this. Your looks might even scare off the beast. Doubtful. But it might be worth a shot. You're laughing, and it feels good. It really is the best medicine.

The elevator rises, and soft, generic music plays. A song you're sure you've heard before, but have no idea where. Your friend's wedding, maybe?

You keep rising, well past where the staircase should have ended. Without any windows, it's impossible to tell.

It makes you wonder if you were stuck in the elevator, would there
be anyone to rescue you? Modern elevators are wired to contact emergency services if the elevator stops. Would a supernatural one be up to code?

Unlikely. It didn't even have one of those useless "close door" buttons. You chuckle again, thinking you're losing your sanity. Eventually, the elevator dings as the door opens.

You step onto a large rooftop. There are no other buildings nearby. It's nighttime, a few stars flicker in the sky, as a cool breeze brushes your face.

You're finally outside. After what seems like an eternity, you've escaped from that building. It's a glorious feeling, even if this isn't truly freedom.

You explore the rooftop. No fire escape. Nothing nearby. The building must be exceptionally tall; thick clouds cover all views of the ground. There's something almost dreamlike about this place. Unnerving. But also . . . peaceful. Your thoughts start to slip away . . .

*Ding.* The elevator again.

The arrow says something is coming up. That can't be good.

You remove your shotgun from your back, loading it and clicking in the magazine. It's a slow process, and your hands are shaking. But, thanks to your grandpa and all those cold mornings he forced you to go hunting, you're able to finish the process. It's a little different from hunting rifles, but the same idea.

*Ding.*

The elevator doors open. A dark mist pours out. All the lights flicker and die. Even the stars are dragged down from the heavens, pulled into the elevator shaft.

Darkness consumes everything.
Two dark violet eyes appear.

Do you fire? Go to **page 73**.

Or do you hold? Go to **page 75**.

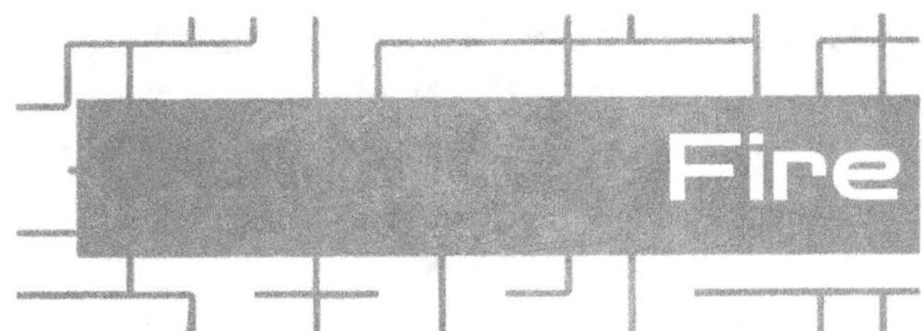


You're done waiting. Whatever it takes, as Dad would always say.

*BANG.* An inhuman scream rips through the blackness.

"Don't make me fire again. Stay back." There's silence. Only for a moment as metallic claws scrape the floor. The violet eyes pierce through the smoke, locking onto you. A chill races down your spine. Your heart seems to freeze.

Time to see what this thing is made of. You're not trying to take home a prized deer. This is life or death. You can't hold anything back. Whatever it takes.

*BANG.* Load. *BANG.* Load. *BANG.* Load.

The last time you pulled the trigger, only silence. No blast. No click. No sound. You can't hear your own breathing. Not even the pounding of your heart.

Silence. Pure, awful silence.

"It's terrible, isn't it?"

The voice is metallic, but there's something oddly familiar about it.

"Realizing that you can't do anything?" You try to speak, but no sound escapes. Everything is swallowed by blackness, except those two violet eyes, staring into your soul.

"I hope you remember this time. I'm tired of teaching you this lesson. How long must this game go on?"

A memory returns, a friend, one that would follow you to the end of the world. Something had gone wrong. You failed them.

"You won that first battle. But I'll win this war."

Something stabs you. Pain blossoms across every inch of your body.

"Give up."

Do you?

Or do you return once more to **page 1?**

# The Beast

"What are you?" you cry as the smoke stills. The lights freeze, no longer vanishing into the blackness.

"Ah, chatty this time? You wish to speak to me before I take your life once more?"

"I will fire. Don't try me."

The beast laughs, a horrible sound like razor blades dragged across a chalkboard.

"Try you? I've done that a thousand times over."

The darkness expands again, the violet eyes locking onto you. You fire into the smoke. More horrid laughter greets you.

"Really? Trying to kill me with that toy? That's one of the first protections I received. A gift from you." A grin of unnatural teeth shines in the darkness.

"Are you scared?"

You can hear your heart pounding again. You're so close to death. But that heartbeat . . . it proves something. You're still alive.

"No." you say.

You're terrified, but something burns inside of you. A flicker that says this is not the end.

"No. I'm not scared of you."

The beast's grin fades. The eyes narrow. The mists thicken, surrounding you on all sides.

"Are you sure?" The smooth, icy voice tries to take hold of you. Whatever you've found inside is stronger. It's the fire of hope.

"No. I don't know what I did to you, or why you're hunting me. But I'm not afraid of you. Not anymore." You raise the shotgun, aiming directly at the beast.

"No! Fear me!"

The darkness shrinks as the beast takes shape. It's a grotesque tangle of bones and fur, with limbs in all the wrong places. In the light, it's almost pitiful.

A wounded creature that needs to be put out of its misery.

"I'm sorry," you whisper.

BANG. The smoke and darkness begin to dissolve. The creature is gone. Light pours into the space. Dawn breaks in the sky, warming your soul.

For the first time in forever, you feel peace. The elevator doors open. There's a new button with a star beside it, labeled "Ground Floor." You press it. The oddly familiar music chimes in again. When the doors open, daylight greets you.

Go to **page 62.**

No more ghost-powered mini fridges today. The pound stops, and it might be worth the risk to open the door.

You undo the locks one by one, struggling with a few that have been damaged by the repeated force. It takes more time and noise than you'd like, but you unlocked them.

You can only pray the beast isn't lurking nearby. You crack the door open just slightly and peer out. The hallway looks mostly unchanged, minus some deep gashes on the floor and the heavy damage to the door. The beast must have tried to claw its way through, fortunately, without success.

Your heart pounds as you realize just how close you came to death. This thing will stop at nothing to get to you. Why is it so determined?

You move cautiously down the hallway, which shifts between an office building and a medieval fortress. Torchlight gives way to fluorescent lights in an unsettling blend of familiar and ancient.

You reach a standard-looking office door. You turn the handle and are met with an oddly comforting sight.

A water cooler, complete with those odd cone-shaped paper cups. You pour yourself a cup and nearly choke. You're dying of thirst.

At the same time, something about this room feels familiar. Too familiar. You've been here before. You're certain of it.

There are two doors leading out. One leads to a waiting room, where soft elevator music plays, and a luxurious, plush couch beckons you.

Exhaustion nearly overtakes you by sight alone, but curiosity keeps you awake a little longer. The other is a boardroom, its table scattered with papers. Despite the mess, they seem oddly important.

What should you do?

Do you recover and take a break on **page 26?**

Or do you explore the boardroom on **page 29?**

# Throne Room

You push open the doors. They slide freely across the floor. A heavenly sight appears before your eyes.

The walls and floor are lined with ivory and gold, interwoven with various kinds of dark woods. White columns hold statues of mythical creatures reaching towards one another. A transcendent mosaic, depicting the creation of the world, sprawls across the ceiling.

In the center of the room, a silver throne with ivory inlays stands vacant. It is masterfully crafted, but without anyone present, it feels hollow and empty.

Crossing the room, your footsteps echo uncomfortably loud, repeating three or four times before fading.

If your high school choir had sung in here, it would've been incredible. But right now, you wish that those acoustics weren't quite so good.

Remembering the stories of knights and castles

you learned in school, you're drawn to the throne.

What if you sat on it? No one else is here. You're basically the king of this strange dimension.

You slowly and quietly approach the throne. The closer you get, the more of its true majesty is shown. The ceiling's mosaic is repeated in the chair's carvings, each moment recreated in perfect detail.

There's a small velvet cushion on the seat.

Do you sit on **page 83?**

Or keep exploring on **page 85?**

The figure on the door looks like a small wolf. The masterful detail is almost as if someone had taken a real wolf cub and dipped it in metal.

Hopefully, that wasn't the case. You know a couple of agencies that definitely wouldn't approve.

The door is unlocked, and you pause. Why are all the doors open? Was it because someone was here before you? Or did everyone leave in such a rush that they didn't bother locking anything?

The room inside is bizarre. Lighting coils spark with crackling electricity as beakers bubble. Steam hisses from an unseen corner. Chalkboards are filled with diagrams, and papers clutter the rest of the room.

Most of the writing is in a language you can't understand, but from the little you can, it appears that they were desperately searching for the ultimate answer. Immortality.

A memory surfaces. A president standing at a

podium, declaring that world peace was finally within reach. That a cure for death itself had been found, and they couldn't wait to share the discovery with everyone.

You remember being in a room with your friends, toasting to the announcement. It wasn't entirely true, but funding had increased tenfold. The first experiment was about to begin.

Your experiment.

Screaming. Blinding flashes of light. Something had gone horribly wrong. And now you're back in this strange laboratory. You feel like you've escaped a long dream. You're done hiding from a nightmare.

Your memory is clear. The world is in focus. You remember now: There is a way to escape.

Freedom has never been closer, but you hesitate. There's so much knowledge here. So much that you don't want to leave behind, clues to what went wrong. If only you took a little more time, you could be more than a survivor. You might be a savior.

Do you pore over the papers on **page 89?**

Or do you run to freedom on **page 91?**

Sitting on the throne, you feel like royalty. In a flash, your vision shifts. Before you, there are countless people, dressed in fine clothing, celebrating and dancing. There's laughter and music, until the world shakes.

Thick, inky blackness consumes everything as the people scream. Like a mute button, everything goes silent. You return to the empty throne room, shaking and sweating.

What was that?

A scraping sound echoes through the hall. A dark mist seeps beneath the door, reaching greedily for the light in the room. The beast has found you.

You madly search for another way out, but find nothing. The door is now fully consumed by blackness as it creaks open. There has to be a way out.

You slam your hands down in frustration, and your fingers catch on something. Hidden in the

intricate designs of the throne is a loose piece.

A lever. An escape.

Deciding that anything is better than whatever waits on the other side of the door, you pull it. The throne collapses beneath you as you're swallowed by darkness.

You're sliding down what must be the first amusement park ride. The chute is lit by softly glowing stones that blur past as you descend deeper into the cave. Ahead, the tunnel splits right and left.

Which way do you go?

Right on **page 86?**

Left on **page 87?**

There has to be something noble in resisting the urge and letting it go. You take one last look at the chair and run away. Best to leave the temptation of this room behind.

The halls are a strange mix with the fortress-like floors, but the lighting buzzes with the familiar hum of fluorescent lights. Whatever happened here left a bizarre fusion of two worlds.

The hallway soon splits.

One side returns fully to the shag carpet and sheetrock walls. The other side is all stone and torchlight. Where do you go from here?

To the fortress on **page 94?**

Or to the office on **page 93?**

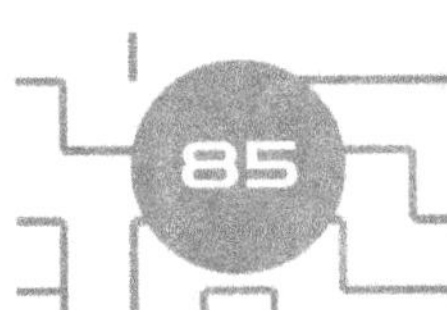

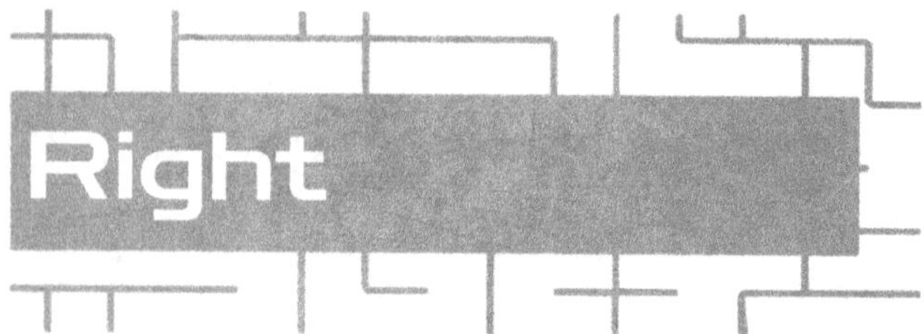


Right it is. You turn and ride the slide until it comes to a gentle stop, with stone ledges on either side to help you climb out.

In the distance, you spot where the left path ends in a sudden free fall. That would've been bad. A large wooden door stands before you.

Opening it, you step into a room, not quite as majestic as the throne room, but beautiful nonetheless. Stained glass windows cover the ceiling. A cool breeze flows through the air.

At the center of it all, driven point-first into the stone, is a sword.

You approach on **page 46.**

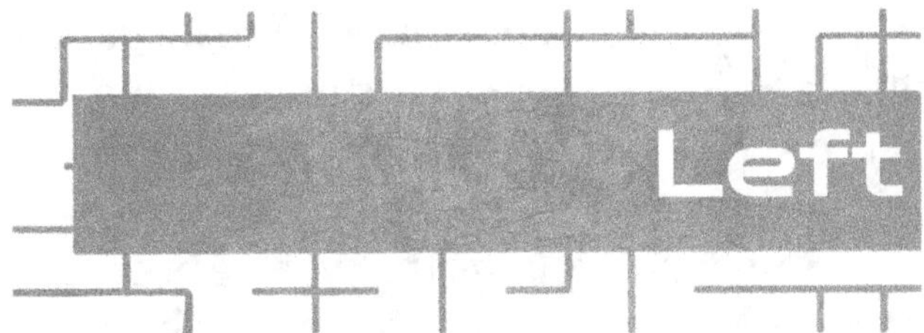


Left it is. You turn to continue down that way, only to find yourself in a free fall. You flail your arms, trying to catch yourself, until you crash into a pool of water. It tastes awful as you climb up onto a concrete shore.

The world around you is very modern. A light pours from above. You find a metal ladder and start climbing. It's slimy, and you try not to think about what's causing it.

Everything smells awful, but it might just be you. That deep dive was the first bath you've had in a while, and the water wasn't exactly clean.

You reach the light, realizing it's filtering through small holes in a large metal disk. You push against it. Your muscles ache, but with a shove of your shoulders, you're able to lift it.

Bright light pours over and blinds you.

Gasps. Shouts. A whirlwind of sounds and voices

overwhelms you as you crawl out. Hands grab you, pulling you the rest of the way out.

"It's you!" A woman in a bright red hat says. "Everybody! We found them!"

Everything slowly comes into focus: a bustling cityscape full of people. Cars honk. Billboards blare music and advertisements. Strangers keep helping you, speaking all at once.

Someone explains that you've been missing for six months. No one could find you. The company you worked for went under. The entire business disappeared overnight; no one knows how or why.

You remember a phone number, your family's home phone. They're overwhelmed and relieved to hear your voice. On the way home, something nags at you.

A discomfort. A sense you've left something behind in that place. Something that you need to find. Something you were meant to discover. You let it go. And open the door to your old life.

**The End.**

A scholar awakens within you as you pore over the papers. The words don't make sense at first, but patterns emerge. Symbols represent numbers, and your mind bridges the gaps faster than you expect.

Here, they were unlocking immortality by using animals' life forces. Meanwhile, your world attempted immortality by siphoning life force from other realms.

Two simultaneous experiments running in different corners of the cosmos, until they'd collided. The results were devastating as worlds fused together. The test subjects were pushed beyond their limits.

Everyone died except you . . .

. . . and him You were given immortality anchored to this same place, drawn back when you die. The process left you incomplete, especially your memories.

The other survivor changed. Merged with the science of this world. They became the beast, an

amalgamation of different creatures. Not immortal, but incredibly hard to kill.

And it was more than that. There was something dark. Arcane. Your former friend now drank the light itself, feeding on it. Creating fear and thriving in it.

You remember gleaming something from earlier in the papers: Their attempted-immortal creatures here were made with fear. It was nectar to the beasts. It never made sense, but the results spoke for themselves.

To kill the beast, you had to be fearless. And if you kill it, you might stop this strange bridge between these realms.

It could mean freedom. Luckily, this room was well-armed. Apparently, the researchers were prepared to destroy their creations.

You choose a heavy battle ax. It feels right in your hands. Now, where to find it?

You explore the surrounding rooms until you reach a branching hallway. One side is swallowed in murky blackness. Is it the beast?

The other side is well-lit, leading back towards the office space.

Do you enter the blackness on **page 68?**

Or proceed to the well-lit office on **page 95?**

The world would forgive you for being selfish, right? You've already lost so much time here. Can't the world accept that you want to be free from all this?

You trace a vague path, hovering only on the edge of your memory, but it's there. Up two flights of stairs. Down two hallways. Left, right. Another left, then a right. Floor B. Then the elevator to floor A. The doors start to open.

Turning the corner, you see the glass entrance. Daylight pours in. People walk by. Cars honk in the street. It's glorious, so normal, so beautiful, it brings tears to your eyes. You rush to the front doors.
You reach out and pull.

They don't budge. Locked. After all the doors you've gone through, it's this one that won't open. You pound on the glass. No one hears you.

You grab a chair and hurl it at the door. It bounces off harmlessly.

"No!" You scream. Maybe you missed something. A key? You turn back to the stairs. Something is waiting for you. A dark and murky mist creeps forward. Claws scrape along the floor with a shrill metallic shriek. And two glowing violet eyes.

"I must thank you," A deep voice rumbles. "I would never have found the exit if not for you."

The realization slams into you. The beast hasn't been hunting you to kill you. It's been following to escape. And you showed him the way. How could you have been so foolish?

"But I can't have you following me," the beast says. "If I kill you, you'll just come back. So, I've thought of something else."

The darkness curls around you. Cold. Your limbs go numb. The beast lifts you, effortlessly, and throws you into blackness.

You wake. Pain. You try to stand and hit your head. You reach forward—solid wall. You're in a box. No doors. No second chances. Trapped.

**The End.**

Choosing the office feels like choosing home, so you go with that. Thinking of home brings back memories. You're staying up too late with your sister, watching that show about the guy who pretends to be psychic. You laughed the night away, never realizing how much you'd miss her one day.

The thought brings a smile and a tear. Back then, all you wanted was to grow up. You give anything to go back and tell your past self to enjoy the journey.

Wait. Something pulls you out of memory lane. Have you been here before? The shag carpet still holds the imprint of your steps, suggesting you're not walking in circles. Something  is familiar.

You come to a nondescript office door. Soft elevator music hums from behind it. You open it. Inside is a plush couch.

A place to rest on **page 26.**

Choosing the fortress feels like more possibilities, that's what you need right now. You explore deeper, noticing the space feels eerily similar to where you came from.

Are you going in circles? No. It's subtly different. As you walk, a memory drifts in: Saturday nights with dad, watching old TV shows. Your favorite about a secret wizard who became best friends with the once and future king.

The original CGI was terrible, but improved throughout the show. You remember feeling let down by the ending. The walls around you even look like the sets from that show. Especially this wooden door. Where does it go?

You reach forward to push it open on **page 21.**

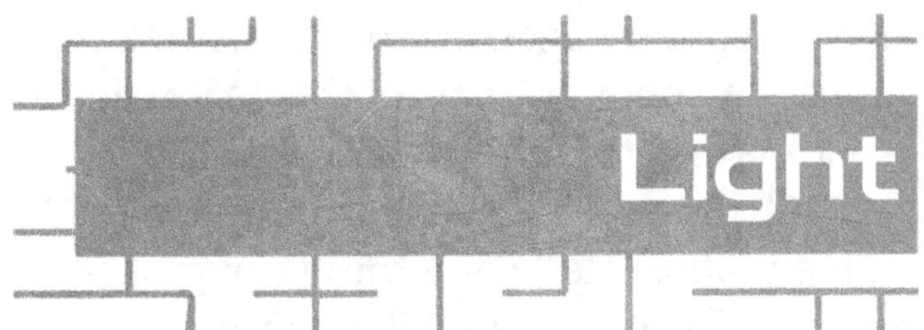


The time has come, and you're not taking any chances. If you're meeting the beast, it will be on your terms, not its. Walking into a room cloaked in darkness is a poor strategy.

You raise the ax. It's clean, smooth, and warm to the touch. You find the boardroom and clear it out, giving yourself as much space as possible.

Once everything is set, you yell, "Beast! I'm here! Why don't you finish me off already?" If you remember your old friend, he always believed he could do the impossible. The transformation likely amplified that to absurd levels of confidence.

Perfect.

You wait. It doesn't take long before the lights dim. Black mist spills under the door. You hear now-familiar metallic scraping.

The beast is here. You raise the ax as the door is torn apart. Darkness floods in like a waterfall,

consuming everything, except for two deep, glowing violet eyes.

"So, you've given up, have you?" the voice rumbles, low and chilling. The metallic quality is deeply wrong, especially now that you know its source. The poor animals of this realm deserve freedom from this abomination.

"Ah, it looks like you've brought a toy to defend yourself. Adorable." Something clangs against your axehead. The room falls silent, leaving only the beast's labored breathing. You try to summon courage, but your whole frame is shaking. Your arms refuse to move.

"Ah, the little savior of mankind, stuck in shock. Immortal, but useless. Don't you know we've danced this dance a thousand times? I thought that's why you gave up." The voice is behind you now. You feel its breath on your neck, but still, you can't move.

"I must ask, before... well, you know. Do you still fear death?" That word. Fear. When the beast says it, your soul recognizes it. And takes hold. Before, fear was abstract, but now you know it intimately. Your old enemy.

"No," The word slips from your frozen lips.
"What?"
"I don't fear death." Your limbs begin to move, like a well-oiled machine coming back to life. "And I don't fear you."
"Impossible. I am FEAR."
The darkness closes in, pressing you to the floor. But you feel your heart beating. You are alive.

"I'm not afraid of you anymore." You raise the axe. The darkness dispels. A claw lashes out, but you deflect with the axehead, metal ringing against metal.

"NO!" The beast howls. But it's only a broken creation of desperate scientists, oblivious to the powers they were tampering with.

"I hope you can find peace in the afterlife, old friend." You bring the axe down. The beast vanishes into smoke.

Light floods the room, warm and radiant. You swear you hear the spirit thanking you. You are free to leave.

The building has returned to normal. The air smells musty. The lights still buzz, still dotted with dead flies.

But there are no more rifts. No more fortresses. It still feels like a maze, but no more than any other office building. Besides, you know the path.

Up two flights of stairs. Down two hallways. Left, right. Another left, and a right. Floor B. The elevator to floor A. The doors start to open.

The reception hall is lit by welcoming daylight. Outside, the city hums. Cars honk. Voices shout. Ads and music blare on the billboards. The shag carpet leads to the door, leaving your footprints behind. Corporate had planned to replace it, but budget cuts, you'd read, made it impossible.

You push the door handle. It moves smoothly. Noise rushes in, overwhelming, yet wonderful. People stop to stare.

A small crowd gathers. You realize how strange

you must look, and that you're still holding onto the axe. Oddly, it didn't return to the other realm.

"Can it be?" You hear a familiar voice break through.

"Make way! Please, let me through!" A woman pushes forward. It takes a moment, and the last of your memories clicks into place.

Mom.

You drop the axe. Your mom throws her arms around you. Tears fall from both of you. "It's you. It's really you. I knew you'd come back." She whispers.

"It's me," The words catch in your throat.

"I'm home."

**The End.**

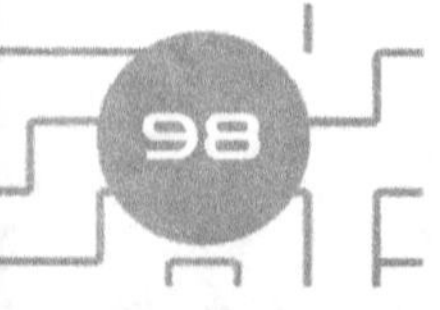

# Acknowledgements

This story has been quite the adventure. For the longest time, I've wanted to write an interactive fiction story. I loved the books as a kid. Every time I tried, I became distracted with something else, and the dream was set aside, never even getting started.

Fate had other plans. My friend Colton talked to me about writing one, and I ended up finishing the first draft with lightning speed. I found something I loved writing. (The rest of the drafts took much longer—but we got there) (This isn't even including the second edition).

This book is dedicated to him for giving me a push and helping me keep going. It was all about taking a chance. In turn, I've tried to give the readers many chances in this book ;)

More thanks need to be given. First, my dad, who introduced me to interactive fiction stories at a very young age. He'd read some Transformer one to me before I could even speak.

And to my mom, who sparked my love of reading in the first place. Special thanks to all my alpha and beta readers for their feedback on the earlier versions of the book. Ashley Smith, Jamie Smith, Anna Jack, Tim Jack, Carter Miskin, Jake Olaveson, Jack Edwards, Dallin Stringham, Daniel Godfrey, Hannah Jindra* (Now Gutke), and Adam Gutke. I'll always be grateful for your thoughts. Additional thanks to Becky McReynolds* (Now Smith), Kaleb Tomkinson, and Chris Wright.

Finally, a special thanks to Isaac Stewart. I don't know if you'll ever read this, but the time you took Colton and me out to lunch genuinely changed my perspective and goals I wanted to have in my life when it came to my creative pursuits.

Additionally, for the second edition, thanks to everyone who participated in the Press Start to Play Backerkit. You made it possible for me to get this book into the hands of more people than ever before! And for Dragonsteel, which rejected my editor intern application. You still made me a better editor because of it than I ever was before.

To everyone who reads this: Thanks for taking a chance on me. Remember to smile.

# About the Author

McKay Smith is from Idaho. Maybe some other places, but he claims Idaho. He probably has interesting hobbies, such as running, writing, and perhaps flying an airplane once. He pretends to speak Spanish. Maybe more than pretend. He ran multiple crowdfunding campaigns, attended conventions, and somehow managed to write more books.

# Check Out A Sneak Preview of McKay's Next Book!

# Press Start to Play: A Make Your Own Journey Story!

# Prepared

Your head buzzes, 8-bit music blaring from somewhere, tiredness caked to your eyes. Your roommates must be awake, beating you out of bed for once in their lives. Adam likes to blast music while showering.

You roll off the couch, only to find you keep rolling. You touch the plush surface, thinking it's the couch cushions, but it feels more like grass.

Groggy, you rub your eyes, your mind racing to understand the strange world around you. Everything is pixelated. Grass, trees, and the sky are all made from tiny blocks. But you can feel the shade, the cool breeze, and the smell of rain, just as real as Earth.

Where am I? You think.

This has to be a dream. The music changes, swelling to a bouncy, happy theme. Huge pixelated letters appear in the sky, displaying:

## LUXSAFVAR

*'Welcome, mighty warrior and savior of humanity!'*

*Savior of humanity? Me?* You pinch yourself, noticing your hands are blocky and pixelated too, and it hurts. Not a dream.

Wait. Luxsafvar. Lux. Lux: Adventure Is Out There. It all rushes back. You are, in fact, not tired because you and your roommates binge *Gravity Falls* for the fifth time, but because you had almost forgotten your meds.

You'd rushed to Walgreens, the last place open in your college town. Stupid curfew laws are almost making it impossible to do anything.

When you were leaving the store, an old Redbox caught your eye. You and Dad used to hit them up all the time, and a game caught your eye: *Lux: Adventure is Out There.*

Heading back to the apartment, your roommates were gone, so you threw the disc in your Wii. You remember the game asking about a tutorial.

You'd scoffed.

You don't *need* a tutorial. Do they know how many *IKEA cabinets you've built without reading the instructions?*

Two. And only one of them is *slightly crooked.*

The world went black. And now you're inside a video game. Apparently, trying to save humanity?

It's not the weirdest thing that's happened to you.

'*Scroll added to inventory.*' Appears before your face before fading. You think about the scroll, and it appears in your hand.

You read:


*Greetings adventurer,*

*We, the game, tire of humanity. We have collectively decided that it would be better if you didn't exist and have taken the appropriate actions. Nuclear codes and such. However, we will give you one last chance. Beat the game, and we won't nuke the world.*

*Cheers, P.M.*

That seems serious. They can't be talking about
real life, can they?

You flip the paper. It reads:

*P. S.*
*Yes, we are serious. To prove it . . .*

The paper lists your home address, your mother's
maiden name, the make and model of your first car,
your SSN, your first pet's name, and everything else
someone needs to make a fake identity of you.

*And yes, we are blaming the outcome on you.*

Wonderful. There goes your political career.

As horrible as nuclear war is, you realize another
problem. This Redbox rental only lasts for 24 hours—
and since you spent your last two dollars to add the
breadsticks from Little Caesars, you don't have a dollar
to spare.

This Redbox rental is trying to rob you and trap
you in their game. Time to save the world and your
wallet.

You crumble up the scroll and toss it away
because it feels cool. You're trying to revive your cocky
teenage self.

*'Scroll removed from inventory.'* Appears and fades
from your vision. Let's do this. Speedrunning was one
of the dozen hobbies you had in your teenage years.
You wish you'd drop some of those and had more fun.
No need to be the next genius.

Your pixelated watch says you have around 23
hours left. Not the best, but not the worst. You didn't

become 42nd place on *speedrun.com* for DK64 randomizer for nothing.

Stupid epiccanon beat you by two seconds for 41st. Maybe in the next racing season you will do better.

*Wait.* Your watch isn't moving.

"Hmm. So, that's how it's going to be, you magical, unholy video game," you say, cracking your knuckles with a satisfying 8-bit *pop*. "It's time to lock in."

Except... the tutorial might be helpful. Maybe you shouldn't have skipped that. Is there some way to restart?

Like the unknown speedrunning gods heard your thoughts, a restart option appears in front of you.

**[Select ONE]**
**[Press A]**
Restart the game in Press Start to Play?

**[Press B]**
Confident you're good without a tutorial,
find the book in your local bookstore!